TO ALL OF MY FRIENDS

Library of Congress Cataloging-in-Publication data
is on file with the publisher.

Text and pictures copyright © 2016 by Aiko Ikegami
Published in 2016 by Albert Whitman & Company
ISBN 978-0-8075-2550-0

Printed in China
10 9 8 7 6 5 4 3 2 1 LP 24 23 22 21 20 19 18 17 16 15

Design by Jordan Kost

For more information about Albert Whitman & Company,
visit our web site at www.albertwhitman.com.

One day...

Aa Dd Ee Ff Ii Jj

A NEW STUDENT CAME.

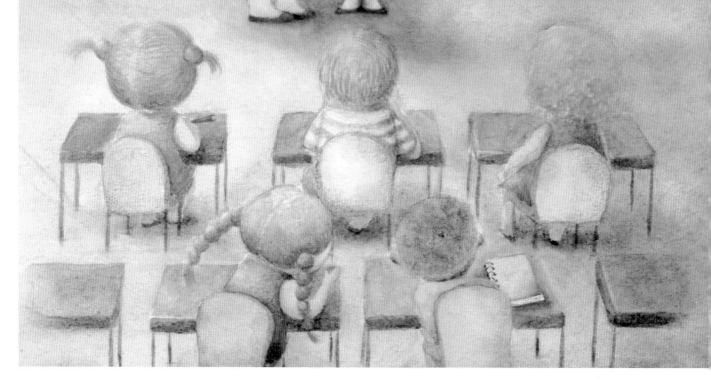

はじめまして

SHE WAS DIFFERENT.

AND ALONE.

SHE WANTED SOMEONE WHO COULD BE A FRIEND.

SOMEONE TO EAT WITH.

ONE DAY...

Someone came to visit.

And stayed to eat.

And play.

Another friend came.

More friends came.

One day...

THEY ALL STAYED TO PLAY.

THEN A NEW STUDENT CAME.

HE WAS DIFFERENT.

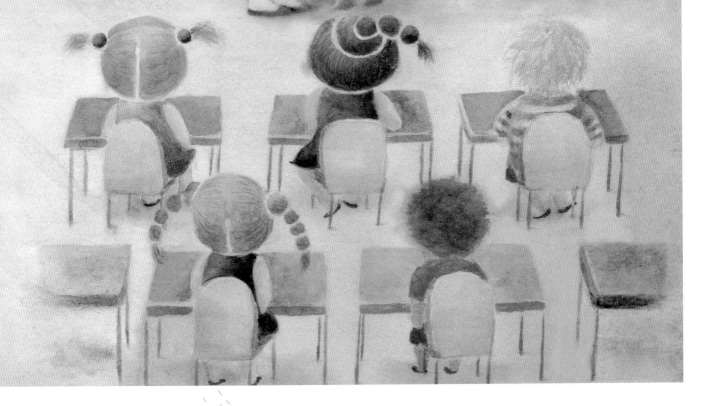

BUT HE STAYED TOO.

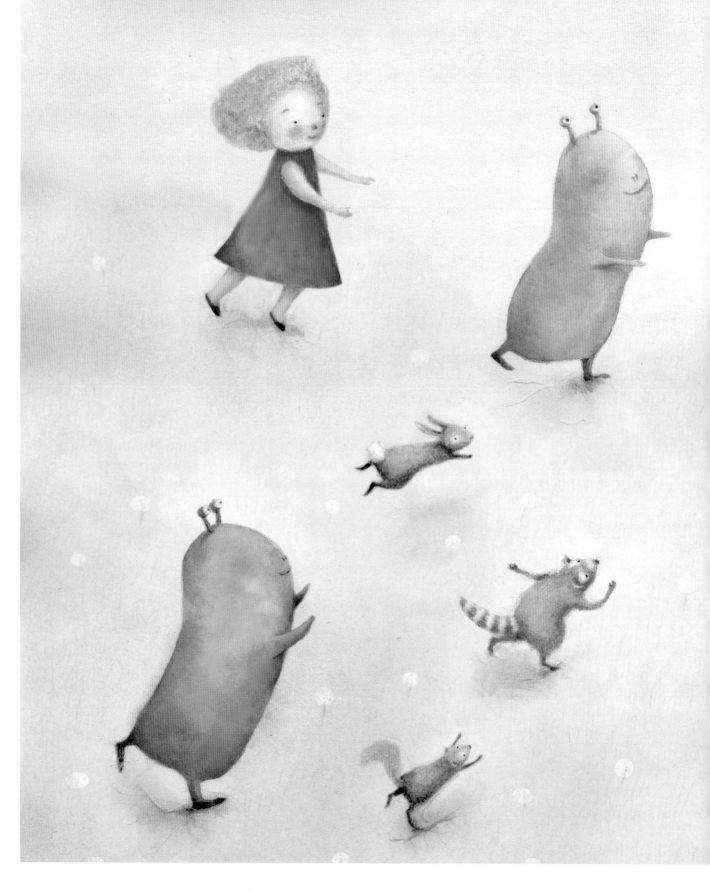

AND THEY ALL PLAYED.